DATE DUE

NOV. 1 4 1984	OC 1 3 '78	
NOV. 2 7 1984		
DEC. 1 3 1984		
JAN. 2 6 1985	AG 16 '9	
JY 6 '8	MR 3 0 '92	
OC 24 '88	NO 16 '92	
JE 16 86	SEP 2 6 95	
NO 13 '8	OCT 0 5 95	
JA 10 '9	AR 2 8 95	
JY 3 '9	JUN 2 4 96	
	AUG 1 3 98	

J
398.22   Storr, Catherine
S   Robin Hood

ROBIN HOOD

Retold by Catherine Storr

Illustrated by Chris Collingwood

Raintree Childrens Books
Milwaukee • Toronto • Melbourne • London
Belitha Press Limited • London

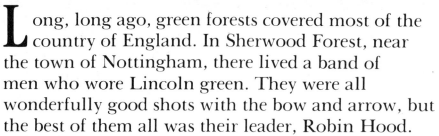

Long, long ago, green forests covered most of the country of England. In Sherwood Forest, near the town of Nottingham, there lived a band of men who wore Lincoln green. They were all wonderfully good shots with the bow and arrow, but the best of them all was their leader, Robin Hood.

Robin had been born the Earl of Huntingdon, but his parents had died while he was young, and he had lost his money and his lands. So he took to the greenwood, and became an outlaw, killing the King's deer for food.

Copyright © in this format Belitha Press Ltd, 1984
Text copyright © Catherine Storr 1984
Illustrations copyright © Chris Collingwood 1984
Art Director: Treld Bicknell
First published in the United States of America 1984
by Raintree Publishers Inc.
205 West Highland Avenue, Milwaukee, Wisconsin 53203
in association with Belitha Press Ltd, London
Conceived, designed and produced by Belitha Press Ltd,
40 Belitha Villas, London N1 1PD
ISBN 0-8172-2109-3

Library of Congress Cataloging in Publication Data

Storr, Catherine.
  Robin Hood.
  Summary: Retells some of Robin Hood's adventures in Sherwood Forest including episodes with Maid Marian, Little John, Friar Tuck, and Will Scarlett.
  1. Robin Hood—Legends. [1. Robin. 2. Folklore—England] I. Collingwood, Chris, ill. II. Title.
PZ8.1.S882Ro 1984   398.2'2'0941   83-24417
ISBN 0-8172-2109-3

3

When Robin fled from his home, he grieved most of all for Marian, the lady whom he had loved since childhood. They had planned to marry. But when he left for Sherwood Forest, Marian had to stay behind, sad and lonely.

At last, she decided that she would follow
Robin to the forest. She dressed herself in
boy's clothes, so that she looked like a young
page. Then she took a sword and bow and arrows,
and she set off alone for Sherwood Forest.

Robin was wandering through the forest. He was disguised as an old beggar. He saw a young page practicing with his bow, and asked, "Where are you going in my forest?"

"Your forest? It is the King's forest," said Marian. She drew her sword, and, immediately, Robin drew his. Then the page and the beggar fought fiercely, though Robin did not use all of his strength because his opponent was so young.

Marian's sword cut Robin's face and drew blood, and Robin wounded Marian's hand. When he saw this, he said, "Young man, for your age you are a good swordsman. Come and join my band and live free in the forest with Robin Hood."

When she heard this, Marian recognized the man she had come to find. "Don't you know me, Robin I am Marian," she said.

Robin took her in his arms. "From now on, we shall fight side by side, and not face to face," he said.

That night the outlaws had a great feast, to celebrate the coming of Maid Marian to Sherwood Forest.

O ne day, Robin was out in the forest alone. He saw an immensely tall man on a narrow bridge across a stream, "Let me pass," Robin said to the stranger.

"Why should I? You should give way to me," said the stranger.

"If you don't let me pass, I will shoot you with my bow and arrows," said Robin.

"That would not be fair. I have no bow and arrows, only my stout staff," said the stranger.

Robin quickly cut himself a staff from a tree nearby. Then he and the tall stranger began to fight on the narrow bridge.

12

ometimes one seemed to be winning, sometimes the other. At last the stranger hit Robin so hard that he fell into the stream. He climbed out, dripping wet.

He blew a loud note on his hunting horn. At once his faithful band of men came leaping through the forest, ready to revenge his defeat. But Robin said, "No, don't attack him. It was a fair fight. This tall man should join our band."

To the stranger, he said. "What is your name?"

The stranger said, "I am called John Little."

"You're much too tall a fellow to be called that," said Robin, and his men laughed. He said, "You shall be called Little John."

13

One of Robin's men was a fat friar. This is how he and Robin first met. Robin was riding through the forest, when he saw a fat man sitting on the bank of a river. Robin said to the man, "Carry me over the river, or you shall pay dearly for refusing."

Without a word the fat man motioned Robin to climb on his back, and he carried him across the river. Then he said, "Now it is your turn to carry me back."

Robin agreed. He carried the fat man across the river. The man was very heavy, and Robin was out of breath when he reached the bank. He gasped out, "Now . . . you . . . will . . . carry . . . me . . . back . . . again."

The fat man hoisted Robin on his back, and waded into the river. But when he reached the middle, he said to Robin, "Now you can swim!" and threw him off into the water.

Robin was angry. He came back to the bank, picked up his bow and arrows and said, "Look out for yourself, fat man!" But Robin's arrows could not pierce the man's steel buckler. So they fought with swords for a long time.

At last, Robin saw that he was going to be beaten. He said, "Grant me a favor. Let me blow my horn for a last time."

"You may do that," said the fat man. Robin blew his horn, and, at once, fifty of his men came running up and took aim at the fat man.

W hose men are these?" the fat man asked.
"They are my men," Robin said.

"Grant me one last wish, as I granted yours," said the man, and he put two fingers to his lips and whistled three times. Immediately fifty hunting dogs came bounding through the trees and growled at the sight of Robin's men with their bows and arrows.

"I see that we had better be friends. Tell me, what are you doing here in Sherwood Forest?" said Robin.

"My name is Friar Tuck. I have come to look for Robin Hood and to join his company," said the fat man.

So Friar Tuck joined Robin's band.

One bleak day, Robin Hood and Little John were out in the forest. They saw a man wearing the dried skin of a horse as a cloak, which seemed very strange to the two outlaws.

"I'll go and find out what this stranger is doing here," said Little John.

"No. I'm the leader. I should go forward first," said Robin. They argued about this so hotly that Little John went off to Barnsdale, while Robin remained in Sherwood Forest.

Little John had just reached the town when he saw another of Robin Hood's men, Will Scarlett, running out. "I've come here just in time," he thought, and he shot an arrow at the crowd chasing Will. The arrow killed the man in

front. But the bow broke and left Little John without a weapon.

Will Scarlett escaped, but the sheriff's men took hold of Little John and tied him to a tree. "You shall be hanged here this very day," said the sheriff.

23

eanwhile, back in the forest, Robin Hood
talked to the stranger. Robin said, "What are
you looking for in Sherwood Forest?"

"I have been sent by the King to punish the
outlaw Robin Hood, for stealing the King's deer.
When I have caught him, I shall blow on my silver
bugle and the sheriff will know of my success," the
man said.

"I will take you where you can find him," said Robin. "But first let us have a shooting competition." He peeled two willow branches and set them upright in the ground. Then he took his place a hundred meters off and said, "Now, come and try your skill against mine."

With his first shot, Robin missed his branch by a hairsbreadth. The stranger's first arrow went near, but not so near. At the second shot, the stranger's arrow grazed the leaf at the top of the branch, but Robin's arrow split his branch into two.

"You shoot wonderfully well. Tell me your name," the stranger said.

"Tell me yours first," said Robin. "I am Sir Guy of Gisborne, a true knight of the King's court."

"And I am Robin Hood."

When he heard this, Sir Guy drew his sword. Without waiting until Robin was ready, he wounded Robin, and threw him down. But Robin leaped up again and fought on, and at last he drove his sword through Sir Guy's body, and the knight fell dead. Robin changed clothes with Sir Guy. Then he blew a single loud blast on the silver bugle. He took Sir Guy's bow and arrows, along with his own, and set off for Barnsdale.

In Barnsdale, the sheriff was ready to have Little John hanged. But when he heard the sound of the silver bugle, he stopped the execution. "That means that Sir Guy has caught Robin Hood. When he gets here, we will have a double hanging, master and servant together," he said. When Robin Hood reached Barnsdale, the sheriff thought that he was Sir Guy. "Welcome, Sir Guy. What have you done with that rascal, Robin Hood?" he said.

"A body with a sword thrust through it lies in the forest, covered with Robin Hood's own cloak of Lincoln green," said the pretending Sir Guy. Then he said, "As my reward, let me ask a favor. Allow me to hang his servant."

obin stepped up to the tree where Little John stood. He took out his dagger and cut the cords. Then he handed Sir Guy's bow and arrows to Little John. Robin and Little John together shot at their enemies till they had all fled.

Then they returned in safety to Sherwood Forest. There, they celebrated their victory with the rest of Robin's band.